THE FIRST MIRACLE

JEFFREY ARCHER

The First Miracle

Paintings by Craigie Aitchison

HarperCollins*Publishers*

HarperCollins*Publishers*
77–85 Fulham Palace Road,
Hammersmith, London W6 8JB

An earlier version of 'The First Miracle' appeared in the collection
A Quiver Full of Arrows, first published in Great Britain by
Hodder and Stoughton Ltd 1980

ISBN 0 00 224595 7

Set in Guardi

Printed in Italy by L.E.G.O., Vicenza

T OMORROW IT WOULD BE 1 A.D., but nobody had told him.

If anyone had, he wouldn't have understood, because he thought it was the forty-third year of the reign of the Emperor. And in any case, he had more important things on his mind.

His mother was still angry with him, and he had to admit that he'd been naughty that day, even by the standards of a normal thirteen-year-old. He hadn't meant to drop the pitcher when she had sent him to the well for water. He had tried to explain to her that it wasn't his fault he had tripped over a stone – that bit at least was true. What he hadn't told her was that he had been chasing a stray dog at the time. And then there was that pomegranate: how was he meant to know that it was the last one, and that his father had taken a liking to them?

The young Roman was now dreading his father's return and the possibility that he might be given another leathering. He could still recall the last one: he hadn't been able to sit down for two days without being reminded of the pain, and the thin red scars hadn't completely disappeared for three weeks.

He sat on the window ledge in a shaded corner of his room, trying to think of some way he could redeem himself in his mother's eyes. He had spilt cooking oil all over his tunic and she had thrown him out of the kitchen. 'Go and play outside,' she had snapped, but playing outside wasn't much fun if you were only allowed to play by yourself. Pater had forbidden him to mix with the local boys.

How he hated this uncivilised country! If only he could be back home among his friends, there would be so much for him to do. Still, only another three weeks and he would . . .

The door swung open and his mother bustled into the room. She was dressed in the thin black garments favoured by locals: it was the only way to keep cool, she had explained to her husband when he had seen her wearing them for the first time. He had grunted his disapproval, so now she always changed back into imperial dress before he returned in the evening.

'Can't you find anything useful to do?' she asked, addressing the sulking figure of her son.

'I was just . . .'

'Daydreaming as usual. Well, it's time for you to wake up, because I need you to go into the village and fetch some food.'

'Yes, Mater, I'll go at once,' the boy said. He jumped off the window ledge, and started running towards the door.

'At least wait until you've heard what I want.'

'Sorry, Mater,' he said, coming to an abrupt halt.

'Now listen, and listen carefully,' she began, counting on her fingers as she spoke. 'I need a chicken, some raisins, figs, dates, and . . . ah, yes, two pomegranates.'

The boy's face reddened at the mention of the pomegranates. He stared down at the stone floor, hoping she might have forgotten. His mother put her hand into the leather purse that hung from her waist and removed two small coins, but before she handed them over she made her son repeat her instructions.

'One chicken, some raisins, figs, dates, and two pomegranates,' he recited, as he might the modern poet Virgil.

'And be sure to see they give you the right change,' she added. 'Never forget that the people here are all thieves.'

'Yes, Mater . . .' For a moment the boy hesitated, wondering if he dared to ask.

'If you remember everything, and bring back the right change, I might forget to tell your father about the broken pitcher and the pomegranate.'

The boy smiled, and clutching the two small silver coins tightly in his fist, ran out of the house into the compound.

The guard who stood on duty at the gate removed a great wedge of wood and allowed the massive door to swing open. The boy jumped through, and grinned back at him.

'I hear you're in trouble again,' the guard shouted after him.

'No, not this time,' the boy replied. 'I'm about to be saved.'

He waved happily to the guard and started walking briskly in the direction of the village, reciting some verses from Virgil's *Aeneid* which reminded him of home. He kept to the centre of the dusty, winding path that the locals had the impudence to call a road. It seemed as if he spent half his time removing small stones from inside his sandals. If his father had been posted here for any length of time he would have made some changes; then they would have had a *real* road, straight and wide enough to allow two chariots to pass.

And Mater would have sorted out the serving girls. Not one of them knew how to lay a table, or even to prepare food so that it was at least clean. Since they had been stationed in Judaea, he had seen his mother in a kitchen for the first time in his life. He was confident it would also be the last. Soon his father would be coming to the end of his tour of duty, and they could all return to Rome.

He had learned many things during the past year, but in particular he was now certain that when he grew up he wasn't going to be a tax collector, or work in the census office.

The village to which his mother had sent him was a few stades from the compound, and the evening sun shone down on him as he walked. It was a large, red sun, the same deep red as his father's tunic, and it was still giving out enough heat to make him sweat and long for something to drink. Perhaps there would be enough money left over to buy himself a pomegranate. He couldn't wait to take one home to show his friends how large they grew in this barbaric land. Marcus, his best friend, would probably have seen one as big, because his father had commanded a whole army in Asia Minor, but the rest of the class would be impressed.

When he reached the village, he found the narrow twisting lanes that ran between the little white houses swarming with people. They had all come from the surrounding area at his father's command to be registered for the census, so that each of them might be taxed according to their rank. His father's authority had been vested in him by the Emperor himself, and once the boy had reached his sixteenth birthday, he too would serve the Emperor. Marcus wanted to be a soldier and to conquer the rest of the world, but the boy was more interested in the law, and in teaching his country's customs to all the barbarians who dwelled in strange lands.

Marcus had said, 'I'll conquer them, and then you can govern them.'

'A sensible division between brains and brawn,' he had replied. His friend didn't seem impressed, and had ducked him in the nearest bath.

The boy quickened his pace. He knew he had to be back in the compound before the sun disappeared behind the hills: his father had warned him many times that they must always be locked safely inside before sunset. He had told his son that he would be safe while it was light, as no one would dare to harm him while others could see what was going on, but that once it was dark, anything could happen. The boy was aware that his father was not a popular man with the locals, but he dismissed the plebs from his mind. (It was Marcus who had taught him to refer to all foreigners as plebs.)

When he reached the marketplace, he began to concentrate on the supplies his mother had requested. He mustn't make any mistakes this time, or he would undoubtedly end up with another leathering from his father. He ran nimbly between the stalls, checking the produce carefully. Some of the local people stared at the white-skinned boy with the curly fair hair and a straight, firm nose. He displayed no imperfections or signs of disease, unlike the majority of them. Many lowered their eyes to the ground when they saw him; he had come, after all, from the land of the natural rulers. The boy did not concern himself with such thoughts. All he noticed was that their native skins were parched and lined from exposure to the sun. He knew that too much harsh light was bad for you: it made you old before your time, his tutor had warned him.

At the last stall, the boy watched an old woman haggling over an unusually plump live chicken. He marched towards her, and when she saw him she ran away in fright, leaving the fowl behind. He looked straight into the eyes of

the stallkeeper, refusing to bargain with such a peasant. He pointed to the chicken, and handed the man one denarius. The stallkeeper bit the silver coin, then peered at the head of Augustus Caesar, ruler of half the known world. (When his tutor had told the boy, during a history lesson, about the Emperor's achievements, he remembered saying, 'Magister, I hope Caesar doesn't conquer the whole world before I have a chance to join in.')

'Come on, come on. I haven't got all day,' the boy said, trying to sound like his father.

The stallkeeper did not reply, as he had no idea what the boy was saying. All he knew for certain was that it was never worth annoying the invaders. He held the chicken firmly by the neck and, unsheathing a knife from his belt, cut its head off in one movement. He passed the bleeding fowl over to the boy together with some local coins, which had stamped on them the image of the man the boy's father had described so often as 'that useless Herod'. The boy kept his hand held out, palm upwards, and the stallkeeper continued to place bronze talents into it until he had no more.

Once the boy had left the man talentless he moved on to another stall, where he pointed to bags containing raisins, figs and dates. The new stallkeeper measured out a libra of each, for which he received five of the near-worthless Herod coins. The man was about to protest, but the boy stared him fixedly in the eyes, the way he had seen his father do so often. The stallkeeper backed away, and simply bowed his head.

Now, what else did his mother want? He racked his brains. A chicken, raisins, dates, figs, and . . . of course – two pomegranates. He walked into the next street, and searched among the stalls of fresh fruit until he found the largest pomegranates on display. He selected three, and immediately broke one open, dug his teeth into it and savoured the cool taste. He spat out the pips, nodded his approval to the stallkeeper, and paid him with two of the three remaining bronze talents (he wanted to keep one to add to Marcus's coin collection when he returned home).

He felt his mother would be pleased that he had carried out her wishes and only spent one silver denarius. Surely even Pater would be impressed by that. He finished his pomegranate and, with his arms laden, began heading slowly out of the market and back towards the compound, trying to avoid the stray dogs that continually ran into his path, barking and sometimes snapping at his ankles. They obviously didn't realise who he was.

When the boy reached the edge of the village he noticed that the sun was already melting behind the highest hill, and recalling his father's words about being home before dusk, he quickened his pace. As he walked up the centre of the stony path, those still on their way down towards the village stood to one side, leaving him a clear path as far as his eye could see (which wasn't all that far, because he was carrying so much in his arms).

But there was one sight he could not fail to notice. A little way ahead of him was a man with a beard – a dirty, lazy custom, his father had often told him – wearing the ragged clothing which signified that he was of the tribe of Jacob. He tugged at a reluctant donkey which was laden down with a very fat woman who was, as their custom demanded, covered from head to toe in black. The boy was about to order them out of his way when the man pulled the donkey over to the side of the road, tied it up to a post and entered a house which, from its sign, claimed to be an inn.

In his own land such a building would never have passed the scrutiny of the local citizens' council as a place fit for paying guests, but the boy realised that for many people during this particular week, even a mat on which to lay their head would be a luxury. By the time he reached the house, the bearded man had reappeared at the door, with a forlorn look on his tired face. There was obviously no room at the inn.

The boy could have told him that before he went in, and was puzzled as to what the man could possibly do next. Not that he was really all that interested: as long as they paid their taxes, both of them could sleep in the hills for all he cared. It was about all they looked fit for.

The man with the beard was telling the fat woman

something, while pointing behind the inn. She nodded her agreement, and without another word he led the donkey off round the side of the building. The boy wondered what could possibly be at the back of the inn, and decided to follow them. As he turned the corner of the building, he saw the man coaxing the donkey through the open door of what looked liked a barn. The boy followed, and when he came to the open door he stopped and stared inside.

The barn was covered in filthy straw. It was full of chickens, sheep and oxen, and smelled not unlike the sewers in the side streets back home. He held his nose, beginning to feel sick. The man was clearing away some of the dirtiest of the straw from the centre of the barn, trying to make a clean patch for them to rest on – a near hopeless task. When he had done the best he could, he lifted the fat woman down from the donkey and placed her gently in the straw. Then he went over to a trough on the far side of the barn from which one of the oxen was drinking. He cupped his hands, and having filled them with water, returned to the fat woman, trying to spill as little as possible.

The boy was growing bored. He was about to leave and continue on his journey home when the woman leaned forward to drink from the man's hands. Her shawl fell from her head, and he saw her face for the first time.

He stood transfixed as he stared at her. He had never seen anything more beautiful. Unlike the common members of her tribe, the woman's skin was almost

translucent, and her eyes shone brightly. But what most struck the boy was her manner and presence. Never had he felt so in awe of anyone, even during his one visit to the Senate House to hear a declamation from Augustus Caesar.

For a moment he remained mesmerised. But then he knew what he must do. He walked through the open door towards the woman, fell on his knees before her, stretched out his hands and presented her with the chicken. She smiled, but said nothing. He offered her the two pomegranates, and she smiled again. He then dropped the rest of the food at her feet. But she remained silent.

The man with the beard was returning with some more water. When he saw the young foreigner he fell on his knees, spilling the water onto the straw, then covered his face with his hands. The boy hardly noticed, but remained kneeling, staring up at the woman. Eventually he rose, and walked slowly towards the barn door. When he reached it, he turned back and stared once more into that serene face. She looked into his eyes for the first time.

The young Roman hesitated for a second, and then bowed his head.

It was already dusk when he ran back out on to the winding path to resume his journey home, but he was not afraid. Rather, he felt he had done something good, and that therefore no harm could possibly come to him. He looked up into the sky and saw directly above him the first

'We do not speak of King Herod,' said the second man, 'for he is but a king of men, as we are.'

'We speak,' said the third, 'of the King of Kings. We have come from the east to offer him gifts of gold, frankincense and myrrh.'

'I know nothing about any King of Kings,' said the boy, now gaining confidence. 'I recognise only Augustus Caesar, Emperor of half the known world.'

The man robed in gold shook his head and, pointing to the sky, enquired of the boy: 'Do you observe that bright star in the east? What is the name of the village on which it shines?'

The boy looked up at the star, and indeed the village below it was now clearer to the eye than it had been in sunlight.

'That's only Bethlehem,' said the boy, laughing. 'You will find no King of Kings there.'

'Even there we shall find him,' said the second man, 'for did not Herod's chief priest tell us:

> *And thou Bethlehem, in the land of Judah,*
> *Art not least among the princes of Judah,*
> *For out of thee shall come a Governor.*
> *Thou shall rule my people Israel.'*

'That's just not possible,' said the boy, now almost shouting at them. 'Augustus Caesar rules Israel, and half the known world.'

But the three robed men did not heed his words, and left him to ride on towards Bethlehem.

Mystified, the boy set out on the last stade of his journey home. Although the sky was now pitch black, whenever he turned his eyes towards Bethlehem the village was still clearly visible in the brilliant starlight.

When he reached the great wooden gate, he banged loudly and repeatedly until the guard, his sword drawn and holding a flaming torch, came to find out who it was that dared to disturb his watch. When he saw the boy, he frowned.

'The Governor is very displeased with you. He returned at sunset, and is about to send out a search party for you.'

The boy darted past the guard and ran all the way to the family's quarters, where he found his father addressing a sergeant of the guard and a dozen legionnaires. His mother was standing by his side, weeping.

The Governor turned when he saw his son. 'Where have you been?' he said in an icily measured tone.

'To Bethlehem, sir.'

'Yes, child, I am aware of that. But whatever possessed you to return so late? Have I not told you on countless occasions never to be out of the compound after dark?'

'Yes, sir.'

'Then you will come to my study at once.'

The boy looked helplessly towards his mother, then turned to follow his father into the study. The guard winked at the boy as he passed by, but he realised that nothing could save him now. His father strode ahead of him, and sat down on a wooden stool behind his table. His mother followed, and stood silently drying her eyes just inside the door.

'Now, tell me exactly where you have been, and why it took you so long to return. And be sure to speak only the truth.'

The boy stood in front of his father and calmly told him everything that had taken place.

He told how he had gone to the village and taken great care in choosing the food for their dinner, and how in so doing he had saved half the money his mother had given him; then how on the way back he had seen a fat lady on a donkey unable to find a place at the inn. He explained why he had followed her into the barn and parted with all their food, how the shepherds had shouted and beaten their breasts until there was a great light in the sky, when they had all fallen silent on their knees, and then finally how he had come to meet the three robed men who sat astride camels and were searching for the King of Kings.

The father grew more and more angry at his son's words.

'What a story this is,' he shouted. 'Do tell me more. Did you meet this King of Kings?'

'No, sir, I did not,' the boy replied. His father rose and started pacing around the room.

'Perhaps there is a simpler explanation as to why your face and fingers are stained red with pomegranate juice.'

'No, Pater. I did buy an extra pomegranate, but even after I had bought all the food, I still managed to save one silver denarius.'

The boy handed the coin over to his mother, believing it would confirm his story. But the sight of it only made his father more angry. He stopped pacing, and stared down into the eyes of his son.

'You have spent the other denarius on yourself, and now you have nothing to show for it.'

'That's not true, Pater, I . . .'

'I will allow you one more chance to tell me the truth,' said his father as he resumed his seat behind the table. 'Fail me, boy, and I shall give you a leathering you will never forget for the rest of your life.'

The boy did not hesitate. 'I have already told you the truth, Pater.'

'Listen to me carefully, my son. We were born Romans, born to rule the world because our laws and customs are tried and tested, and have always been based on complete integrity. Romans never lie; that is our strength and the weakness of our enemies. That is why we rule while others are willing to be ruled, and as long as that is so, the Roman Empire will never fall. Do you understand what I am saying to you, boy?'

'Yes, Pater, I understand.'

'Then you will also understand why it is imperative always to tell the truth, whatever the consequences.'

'Yes, Pater, I do. But I have already told you the truth.'

'Then there is no hope for you,' said the man quietly. 'You leave me no choice as to how I will have to deal with you.'

The boy's mother raised her hand, wanting to come to her son's aid, but knew any protest would be useless. The Governor rose from his chair, removed the leather belt from around his waist and folded it double, with the heavy brass studs on the outside. He then ordered his son to bend down and touch his toes. The young boy obeyed without hesitation, and his father raised the belt above his head and brought it down on the child with all the strength he could muster. The boy didn't once flinch or murmur as

each stroke was administered, while his mother turned away and wept.

After the father had delivered the twelfth stroke he ordered his son to go to his room. The boy left without a word and climbed the stairs to his bedroom. His mother followed. As she passed the kitchen, she stepped in and took some olive oil and ointments from a drawer.

She carried the little jars up to the boy's room, where she found him already in bed. She went over to his side, sat on the edge of the bed and pulled the sheet back. She told him to turn onto his chest while she prepared the oils. Then she gently removed his night tunic, for fear of adding to his pain. She stared down at his naked body in disbelief.

The boy's skin was unmarked.

She ran her fingers gently over her son's unblemished body, and found it as smooth as if he had just bathed. She turned him over. There was no mark on him anywhere. Quickly she slipped his tunic back on and covered him with the sheet.

'Say nothing of this to your father,' she said, 'and remove the memory of it from your mind forever.'

'Yes, Mater.'

The mother leaned over and blew out the candle by the side of his bed, gathered up the unused oils and tiptoed to the door. At the threshold, she turned in the dim light to look back at her son and said: 'Now I know you were telling the truth, Pontius.'

✳

Paintings by Craigie Aitchison

'The Pomegranate' (1994, oil on board)
By courtesy of Thomas Gibson Fine Art

'Gorgeous Macaulay in a Uniform' (1969, oil on canvas)
Collection of Dr Bethel Solomons

'Boy Walking' (1994, oil on canvas)
By courtesy of Thomas Gibson Fine Art

'Donkey' (1993, oil on canvas)
By courtesy of Thomas Gibson Fine Art

'Nativity' (1959, oil on canvas)
Collection of John Lessore

'Sheep at Tulliallan' (1963, oil on board)
Collection of Michael Palmer

'The Three Kings' (1994, oil on canvas)
By courtesy of Thomas Gibson Fine Art

'Donkey Candle' (1993, oil on canvas)
By courtesy of Thomas Gibson Fine Art

'Crucifixion' (1959, oil on canvas)
Arts Council of Great Britain